GREEN TIGER PRESS
Simon & Schuster Building, Rockefeller Center
1230 Avenue of the Americas, New York, New York 10020
Text copyright © 1989 by Welleran Poltarnees
Illustrations copyright © 1989 by Paul Cline
GREEN TIGER PRESS is an imprint of Simon & Schuster.
Manufactured in Hong Kong.

10 9 8 7 6 5 4 3 2

Library of Congress Cataloging-in-Publication Data
Poltarnees, Welleran. Amy and Nathaniel / by Welleran Poltarnees :
pictures by Paul Cline. p. cm. First published in 1989.
Summary: To the delight of their teacher and classmates,
Amy and Nathaniel create several imaginative
bulletin boards during the school year.
[1. Bulletin boards—Fiction. 2. Schools—Fiction. 3. Animals—Fiction.]
I. Cline, Paul, ill. II. Title.
[PZ7.P7694A83 1991]
[E]—dc20 91-22297 CIP AC

ISBN: 0-671-75269-3

Amy and Nathaniel

by Welleran Poltarnees

pictures by Paul Cline

GREEN TIGER PRESS
Published by Simon & Schuster
New York London Toronto Sydney Tokyo Singapore

"I'm glad to have you all here in my class. I know we're going to have a fine year together.

We're going to learn a great deal, but that won't keep us from having fun, too.

I need one boy and one girl to do our monthly bulletin boards. Who volunteers?

Well, I'll have to appoint them, since no one volunteers.

I'll choose ... you, Amy ... and you, Nathaniel. Please stay after school for a few minutes and I'll show you what's involved.

I want you to decorate this board at the beginning of every month. I will help you think up themes to fit the month.

Everything you need should be in here. If you need something you can't find, let me know. Use your imagination."

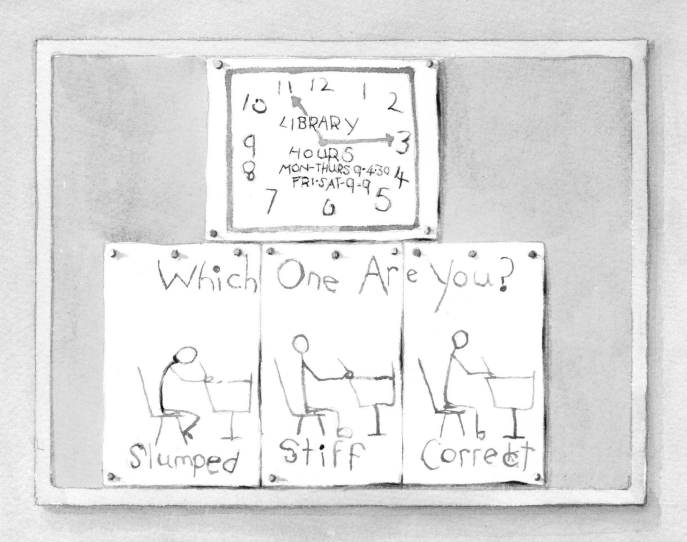

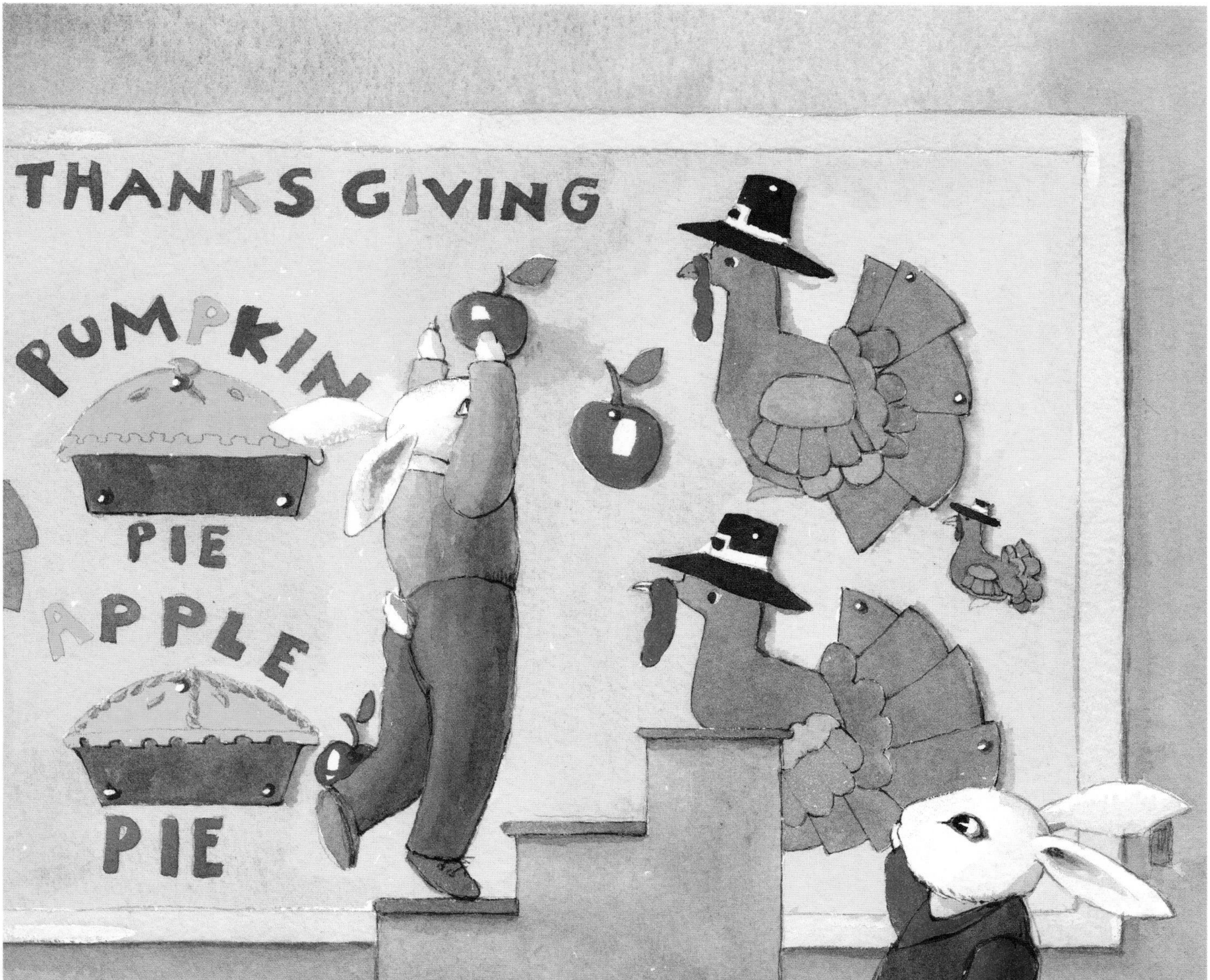
THANKSGIVING
PUMPKIN
PIE
APPLE
PIE

"Now we say goodbye to the old year ..."

OUT WITH the OLD

"I'm turning out the lights for a few minutes,
so be patient."

"It's so dark in here"

"What's happening?"

"Hush, children."

"… and welcome the New Year!"

BECKY
GRETA
SAM
BUD
FRED
CELIA
BARRY
RITA
PAUL
JOHN
PAT
AMY
NAT
our love
teacher
each
HAPPY
VALEN

"Amy and Nathaniel, I want you to know how much all of us have
appreciated your most imaginative bulletin boards. In all my years of

teaching I've never had bulletin board helpers who contributed so much to our enjoyment of the school year. You deserve hearty congratulations!"

"I'm glad to have you all here in my class. I know we're going to have a fine year together.

I need one boy and one girl to do our monthly bulletin boards.
Who volunteers?

Well, I'll have to appoint them, since no one volunteers.

I'll choose ... you, Victoria ... and you, Edward. Please stay after school for a few minutes and I'll show you what's involved."